fin
AF595916
watch out!
great white
hammerhead

splash!
dolphin
squeak!

weee!
orca
Click!
killer whale

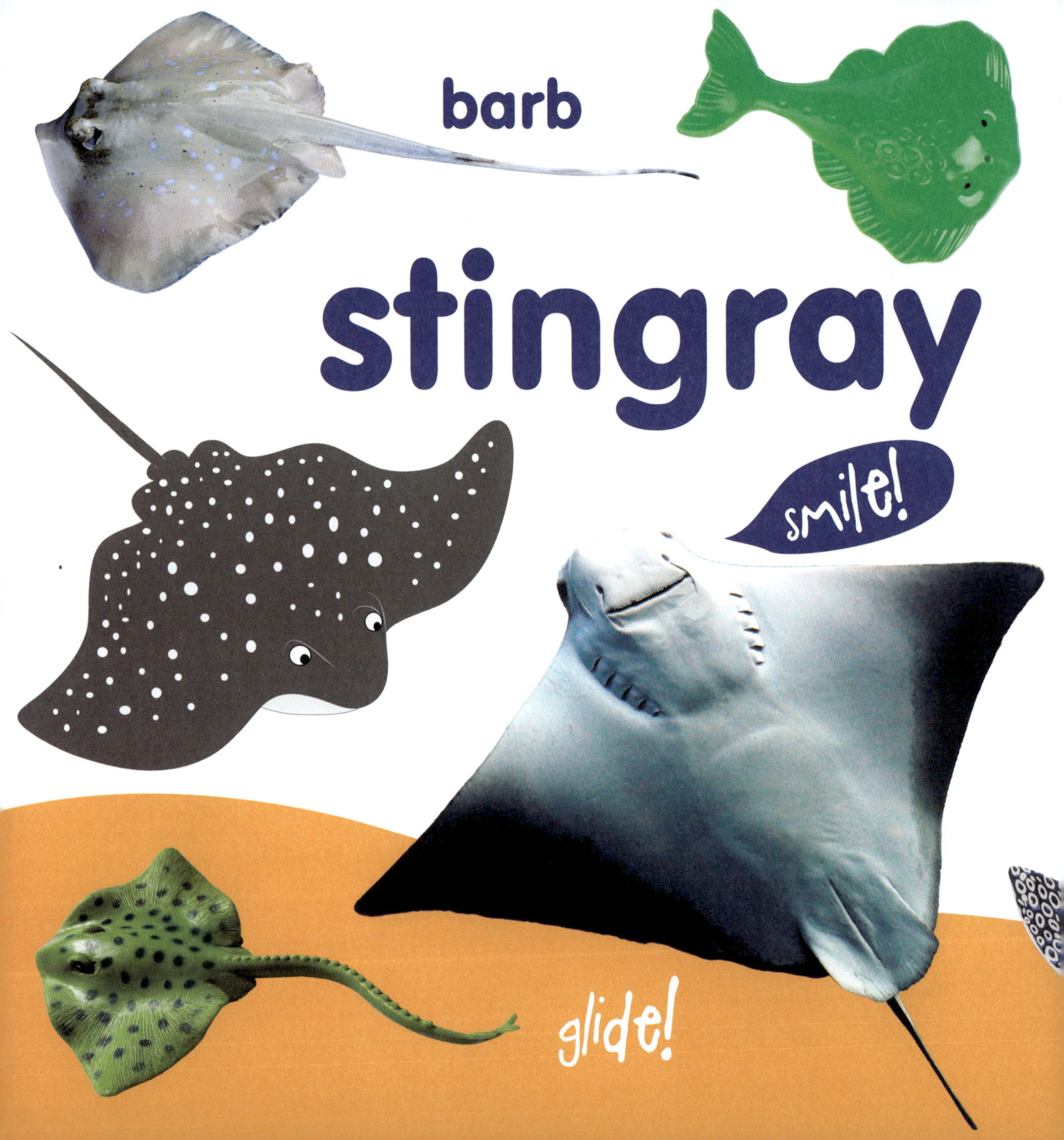
barb
stingray
smile!
glide!

manta ray
Yum Plankton!
eagle ray

squeak!
turtle
egg

jellyfish
jiggle! jiggle!
YUM!

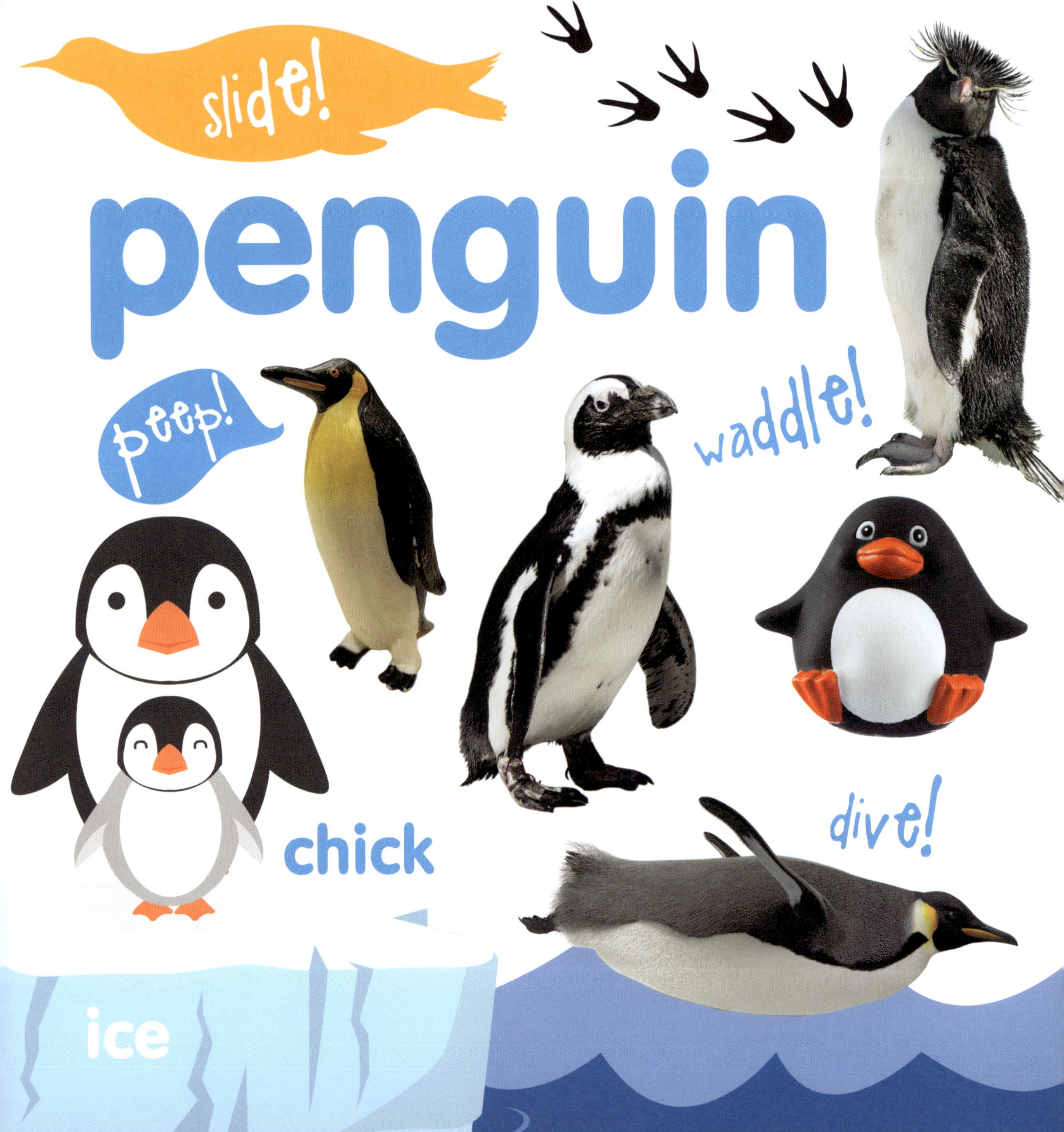
slide!
penguin
peep!
waddle!
chick
dive!
ice

heron
eagle
chick
fly!
nest
bird
albatross
squawk!
seagull
pelican

squirt!
squid
tentacles
ink

suckers
octopus
arms

fins
fish
fishbowl

bubbles
scales

wow!
sea star
starfish
spines

seahorse
sea
dragon
tail

ears
seal
sea lion
pup
arf!

wobble!
tusks
wobble!
walrus
blubber

claw
snap!
crab
snap!
hermit crab

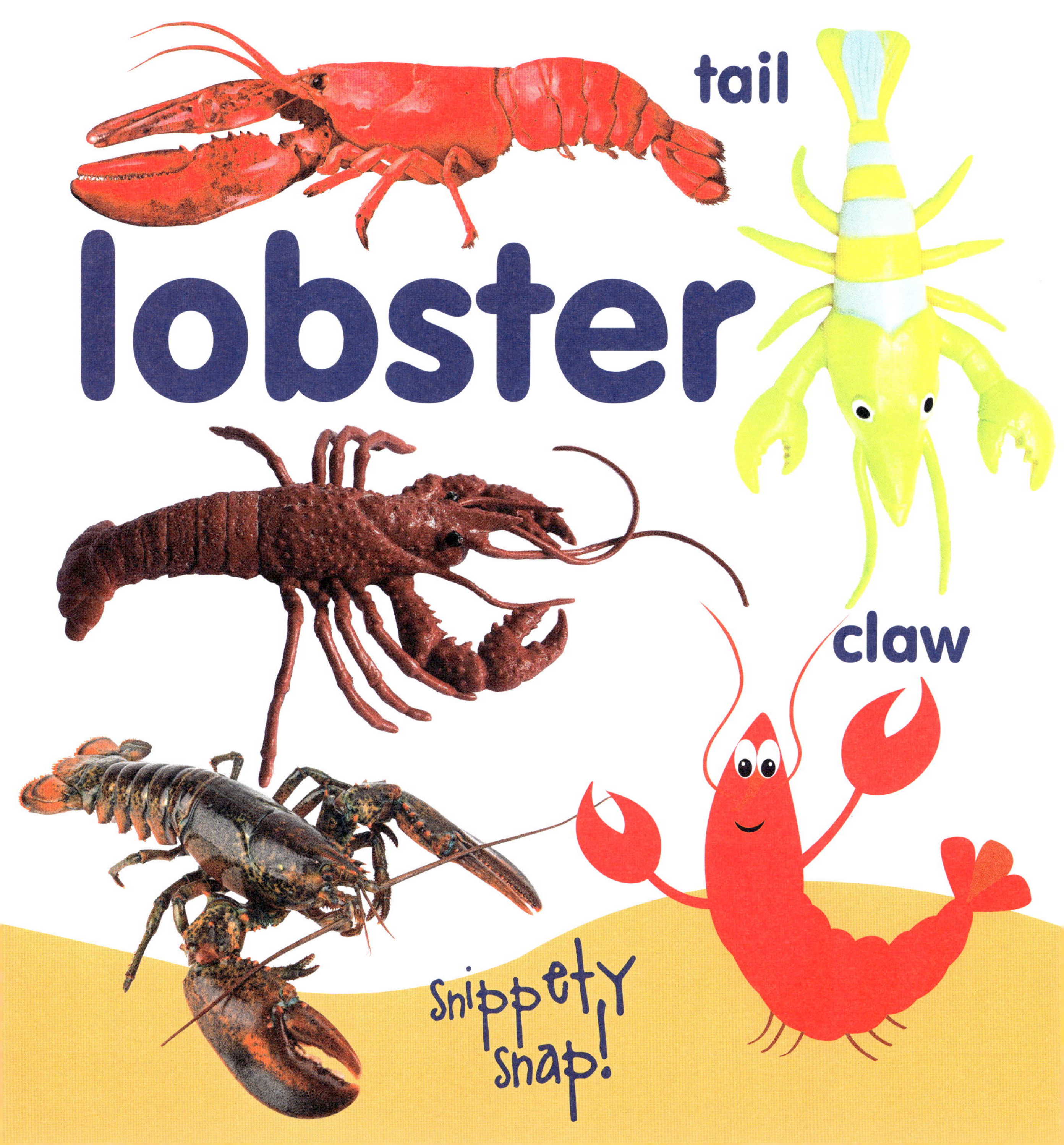
tail
lobster
claw
snippety snap!

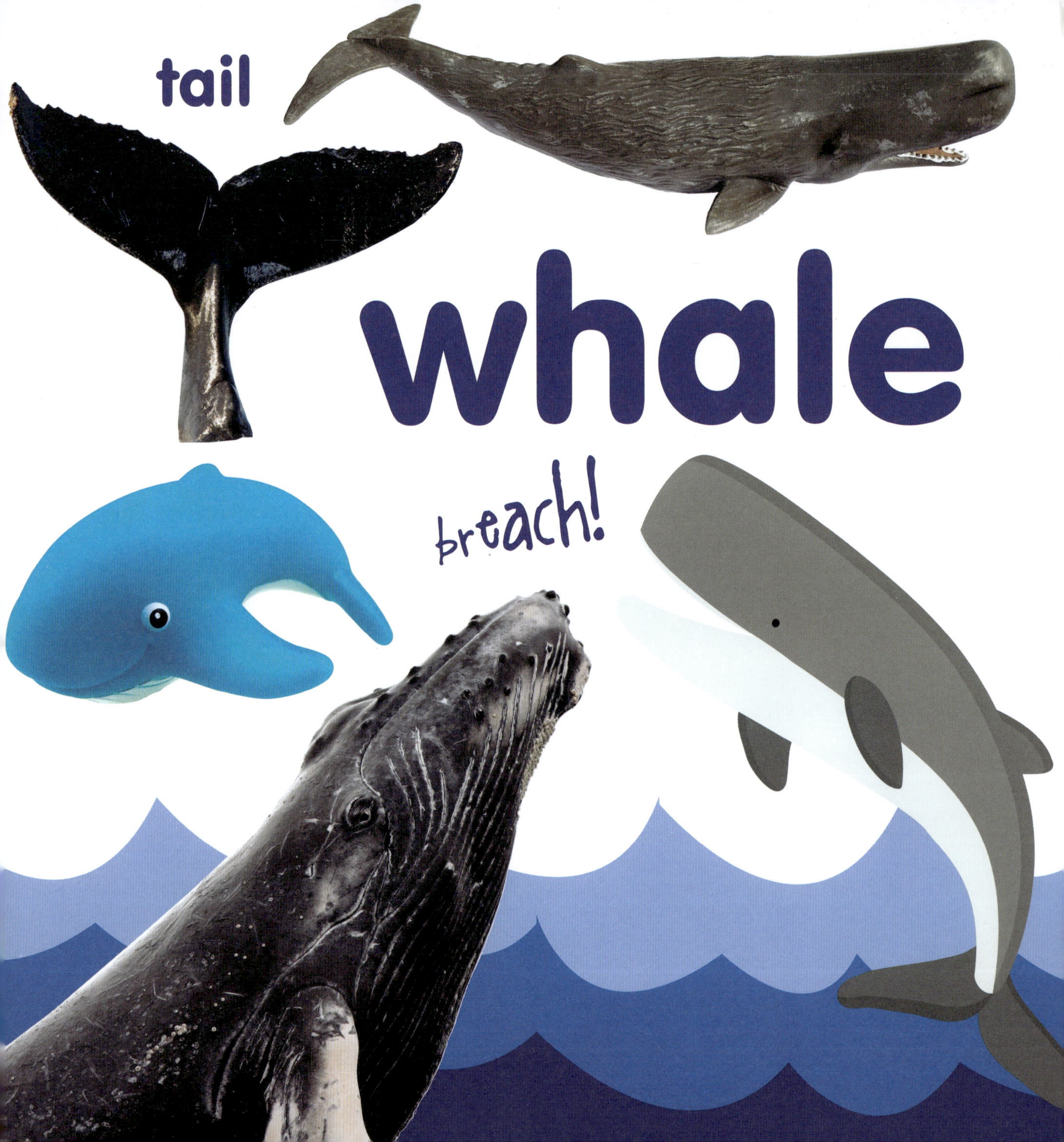
tail
whale
breach!